W9-AHH-064

THE MAN IN THE IRON MASK

Vol. 5: The Death of a Titan

Adapted from the novel by ALEXANDRE DUMAS

THE STORY SO FAR:

In the early 17th century, **Athos**, **Porthos**, **and Aramis**—famed in France
"The Three Musketeers"—were joined in friendship by young **d'Artagnan**. Three
ades later, Athos had become a count—Porthos, by marriage, a baron—and shrewd
mis, the Bishop of Vannes—while d'Artagnan now commanded the Musketeers.

When Aramis learned that **Philippe**, a prisoner in the Bastille, was in fact the
of **King Louis XIV**, held in seclusion since birth, he devised a conspiracy to set
former upon the throne. In this he was unwittingly aided by Porthos and **Nicholas**
uquet, the nation's Surintendant (chief tax collector).

But the scheme failed… Philippe was sentenced to be imprisoned, wearing an
mask…and Aramis and Porthos fled to Fouquet's fortified island called Belle-Isle.
ey paused to bid farewell to Athos and his lovesick son, **Raoul**, who was leaving to find
y—and death—in Africa. And it was Captain d'Artagnan whom the King sent in
suit of Aramis and Porthos….

Writer	Special Thanks		Penciler	Inker
Roy Thomas	**Deborah Sherer & Freeman Henry**		**Hugo Petrus**	**Tom Palmer**
Colorist	Letterer	Cover	Special Thanks	Production
June Chung	**Virtual Calligraphy's Joe Caramagna**	**Marko Djurdjevic**	**Chris Allo**	**Irene Lee**
Assistant Editor	Associate Editor	Editor	Editor in Chief	Publisher
auren Sankovitch	**Nicole Boose**	**Ralph Macchio**	**Joe Quesada**	**Dan Buckley**

VISIT US AT
www.abdopublishing.com

Reinforced library bound edition published in 2009 by Spotlight, a division of the ABDO Group, 8000 West 78th Street, Edina, Minnesota 55439. Spotlight produces high-quality reinforced library bound editions for schools and libraries. Published by agreement with Marvel Characters, Inc.

Library of Congress Cataloging-in-Publication Data

Thomas, Roy, 1940-
The man in the iron mask / adapted from the novel by Alexandre Dumas ; Roy Thomas, writer ; Hugo Petrus, penciler ; Tom Palmer, inker ; Virtual Calligraphy's Jo Caramagna, letterer ; June Chung, colorist. -- Reinforced library bound ed.
v. cm.
"Marvel."
Contents: v. 1. The three musketeers -- v. 2. High treason -- v. 3. The iron mask -- v 4. The man in the iron mask -- v. 5. The death of a titan -- v. 6. Musketeers no more.
ISBN 9781599615943 (v. 1) -- ISBN 9781599615950 (v. 2) -- ISBN 978159961596 (v. 3) -- ISBN 9781599615974 (v. 4) -- ISBN 9781599615981 (v. 5) -- ISBN 9781599615998 (v. 6)
Summary: Retells, in comic book format, Alexandre Dumas' tale of political intrigu romance, and adventure in seventeenth-century France.
[1. Dumas, Alexandre, 1802-1870.--Adaptations. 2. Graphic novels. 3. Adventure and adventurers--Fiction. 4. France--History--Louis XIII, 1610-1643--Fiction.] I. Dumas, Alexandre, 1802-1870. II. Petrus, Hugo. VI. Title.
PZ7.7.T518 Man 2009
[Fic]--dc22 2008035321

Spotlight

All Spotlight books have reinforced library bindings and are manufactured in the United States of America.

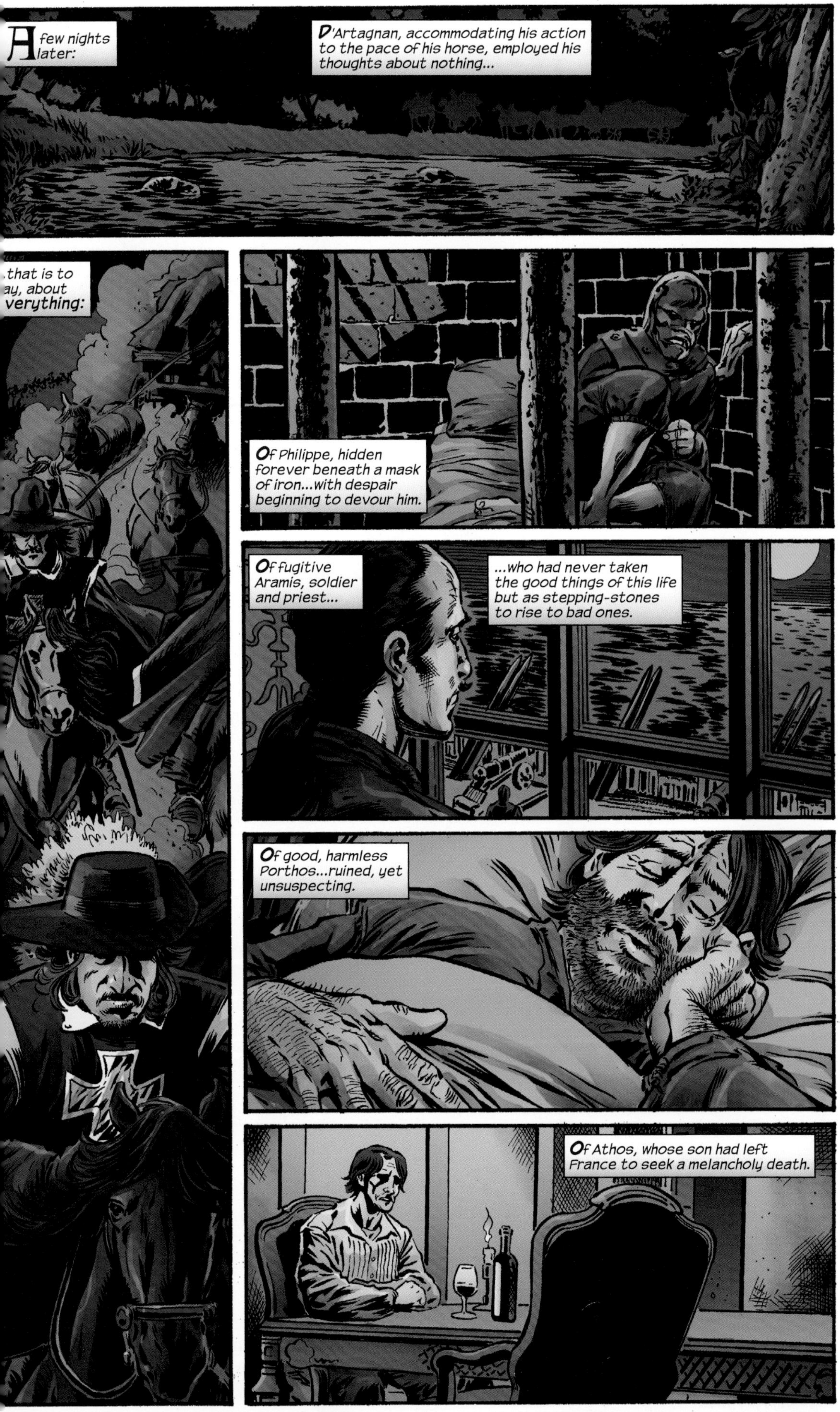
A few nights later:
D'Artagnan, accommodating his action to the pace of his horse, employed his thoughts about nothing...
that is to say, about everything:
Of Philippe, hidden forever beneath a mask of iron...with despair beginning to devour him.
Of fugitive Aramis, soldier and priest...
...who had never taken the good things of this life but as stepping-stones to rise to bad ones.
Of good, harmless Porthos...ruined, yet unsuspecting.
Of Athos, whose son had left France to seek a melancholy death.

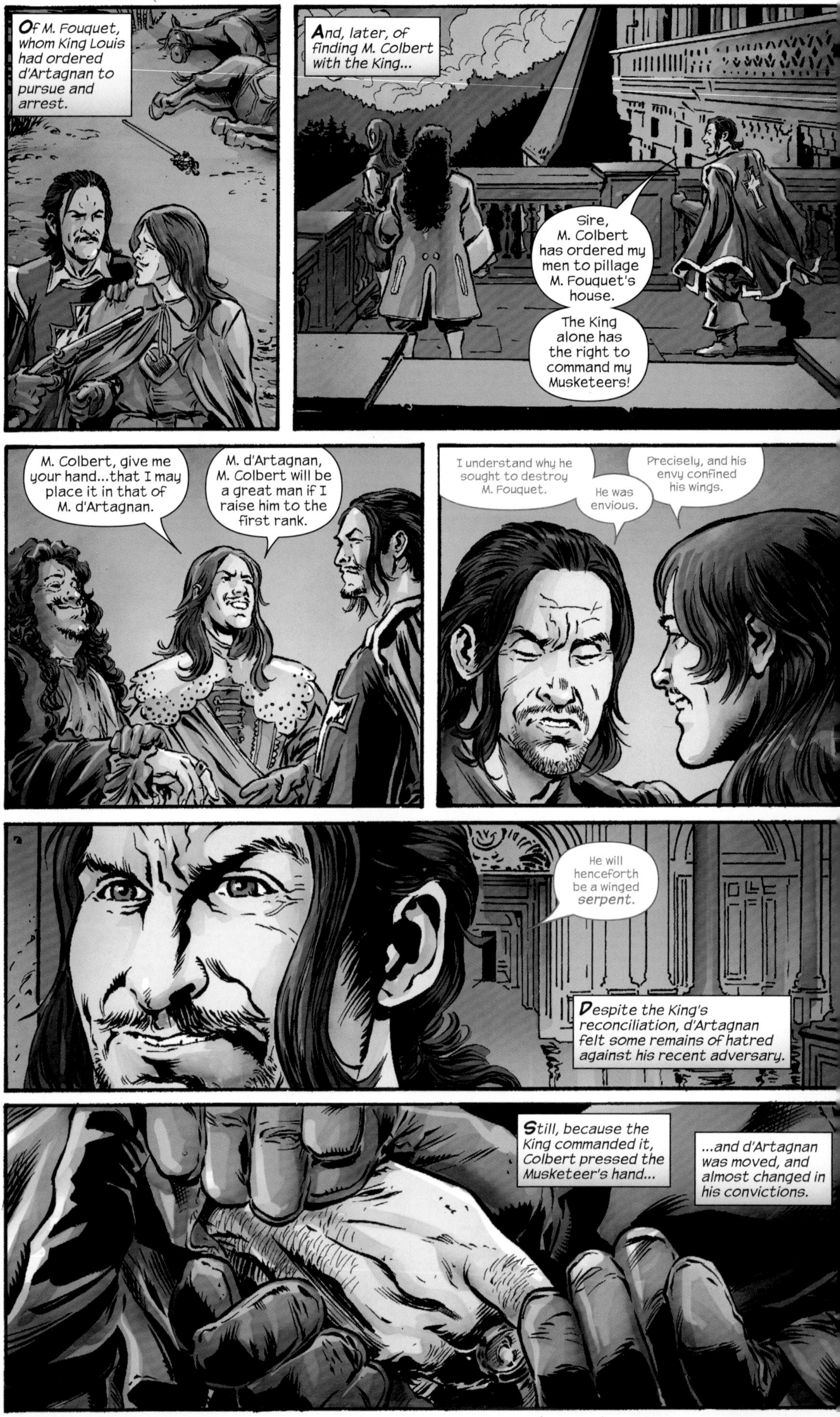

Of M. Fouquet, whom King Louis had ordered d'Artagnan to pursue and arrest.
And, later, of finding M. Colbert with the King...
Sire, M. Colbert has ordered my men to pillage M. Fouquet's house.
The King alone has the right to command my Musketeers!
M. Colbert, give me your hand...that I may place it in that of M. d'Artagnan.
M. d'Artagnan, M. Colbert will be a great man if I raise him to the first rank.
I understand why he sought to destroy M. Fouquet.
He was envious.
Precisely, and his envy confined his wings.
He will henceforth be a winged serpent.
Despite the King's reconciliation, d'Artagnan felt some remains of hatred against his recent adversary.
Still, because the King commanded it, Colbert pressed the Musketeer's hand...
...and d'Artagnan was moved, and almost changed in his convictions.

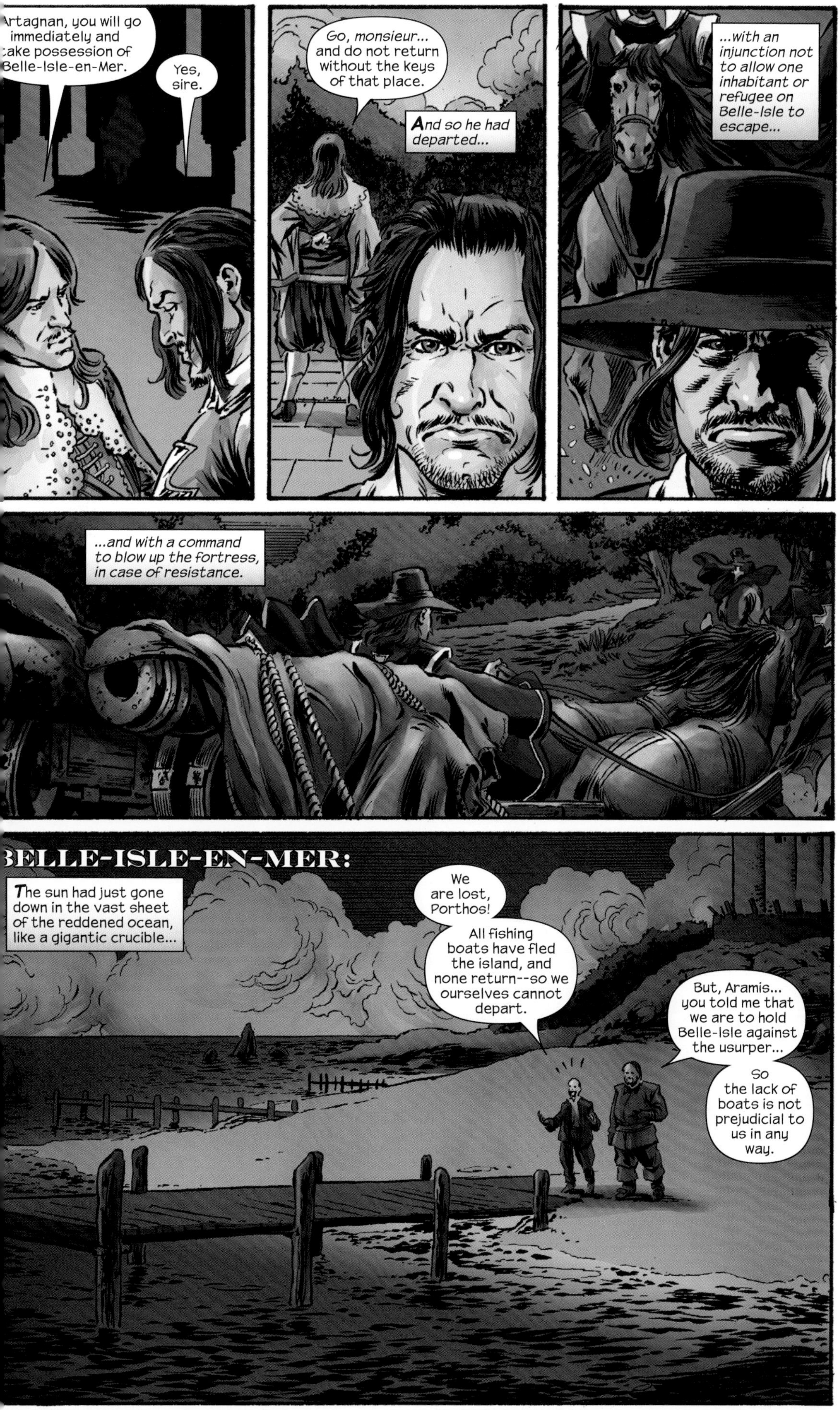
Artagnan, you will go immediately and take possession of Belle-Isle-en-Mer.
Yes, sire.
Go, monsieur... and do not return without the keys of that place.
And so he had departed...
...with an injunction not to allow one inhabitant or refugee on Belle-Isle to escape...
...and with a command to blow up the fortress, in case of resistance.
BELLE-ISLE-EN-MER:
The sun had just gone down in the vast sheet of the reddened ocean, like a gigantic crucible...
We are lost, Porthos!
All fishing boats have fled the island, and none return--so we ourselves cannot depart.
But, Aramis... you told me that we are to hold Belle-Isle against the usurper...
So the lack of boats is not prejudicial to us in any way.

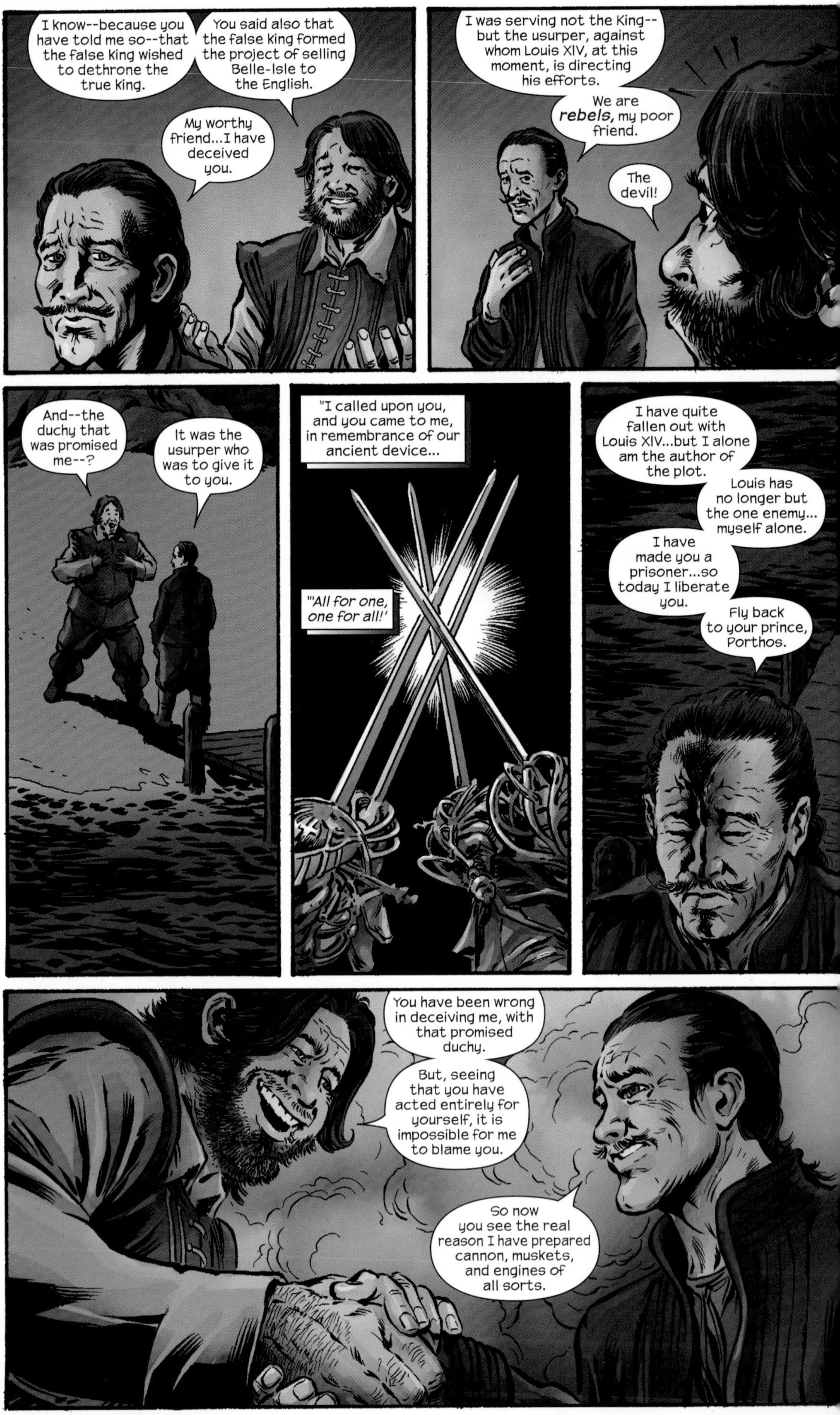
I know--because you have told me so--that the false King wished to dethrone the true King.
You said also that the false King formed the project of selling Belle-Isle to the English.
My worthy friend...I have deceived you.
I was serving not the King--but the usurper, against whom Louis XIV, at this moment, is directing his efforts.
We are *rebels,* my poor friend.
The devil!
And--the duchy that was promised me--?
It was the usurper who was to give it to you.
"I called upon you, and you came to me, in remembrance of our ancient device...
"*All for one, one for all!*'
I have quite fallen out with Louis XIV...but I alone am the author of the plot.
Louis has no longer but the one enemy... myself alone.
I have made you a prisoner...so today I liberate you.
Fly back to your prince, Porthos.
You have been wrong in deceiving me, with that promised duchy.
But, seeing that you have acted entirely for yourself, it is impossible for me to blame you.
So now you see the real reason I have prepared cannon, muskets, and engines of all sorts.

But hark! I hear a hail for landing at the port.

It is d'Artagnan!

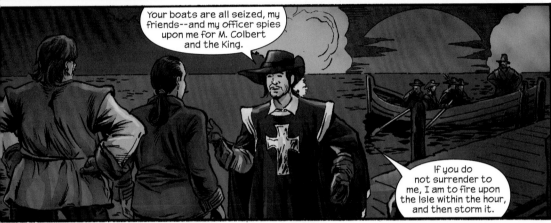

Your boats are all seized, my friends--and my officer spies upon me for M. Colbert and the King.

If you do not surrender to me, I am to fire upon the Isle within the hour, and then storm it.

We must remain at Belle-Isle.

I assure you, d'Artagnan, I will not surrender easily.

Let us say *adieu*, then.

But in truth, Porthos, *you* ought to go with him.

No. I will remain here.

Good-bye, old comrades.

And so d'Artagnan left Belle-Isle with the inseparable companion M. Colbert had given him.

But the captain of Musketeers had discovered an idea...

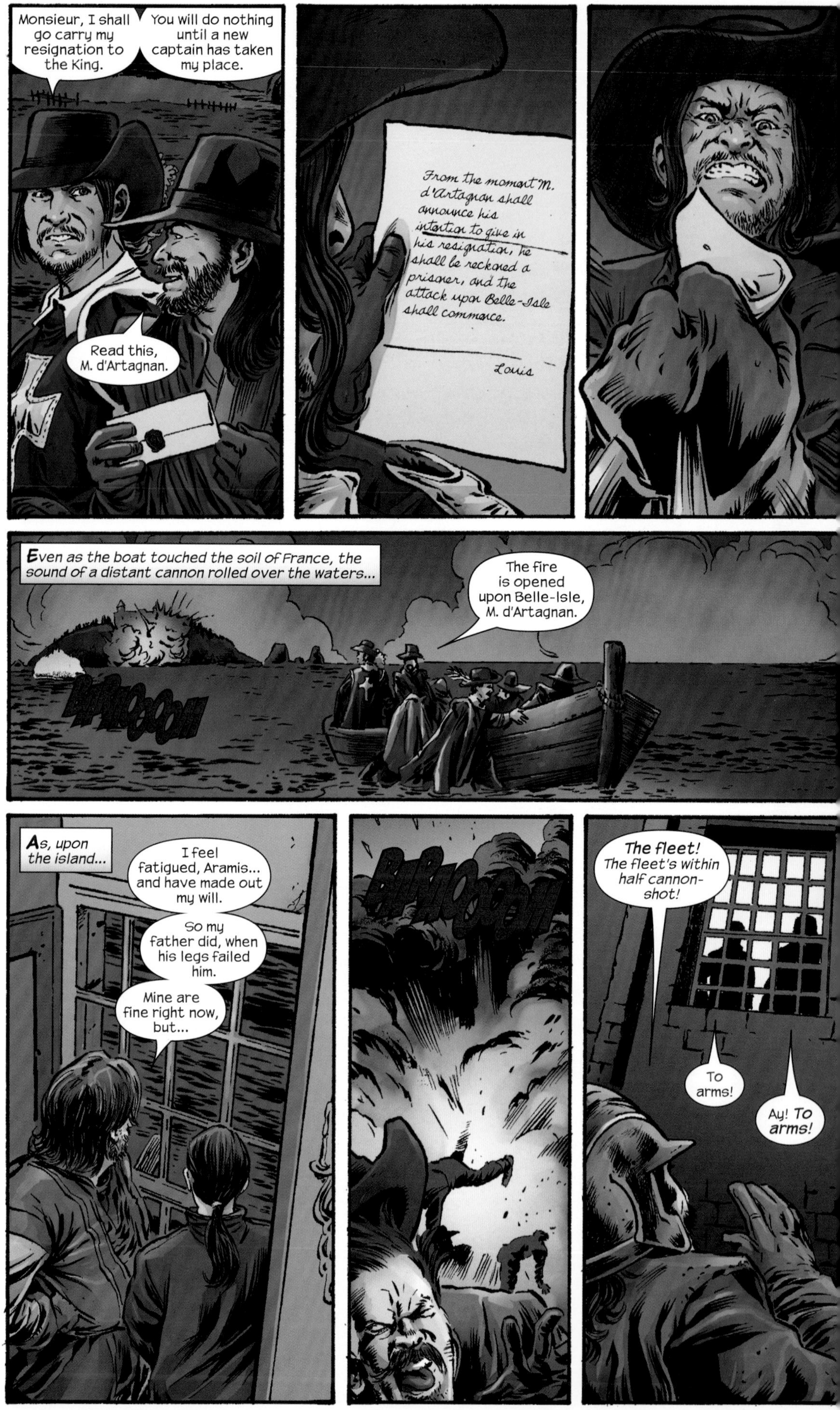

Monsieur, I shall go carry my resignation to the King.
You will do nothing until a new captain has taken my place.
Read this, M. d'Artagnan.
From the moment M. d'Artagnan shall announce his intention to give in his resignation, he shall be reckoned a prisoner, and the attack upon Belle-Isle shall commence.
Louis
Even as the boat touched the soil of France, the sound of a distant cannon rolled over the waters...
The fire is opened upon Belle-Isle, M. d'Artagnan.
BVRROOOM
As, upon the island...
I feel fatigued, Aramis... and have made out my will.
So my father did, when his legs failed him.
Mine are fine right now, but...
BVRROOOM
The fleet! The fleet's within half cannon-shot!
To arms!
Ay! To arms!

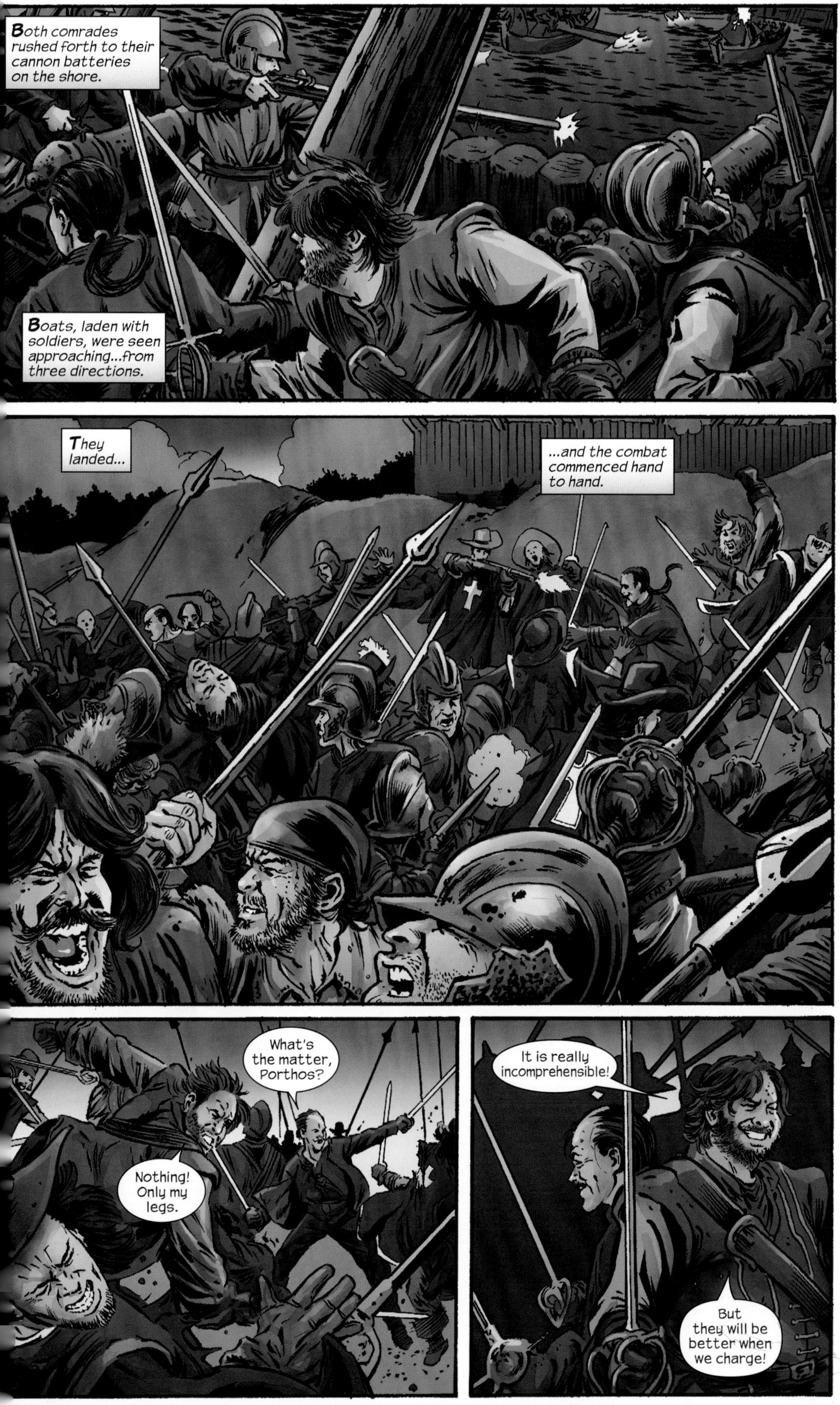

Both comrades rushed forth to their cannon batteries on the shore.
Boats, laden with soldiers, were seen approaching...from three directions.
They landed...
...and the combat commenced hand to hand.
What's the matter, Porthos?
Nothing! Only my legs.
It is really incomprehensible!
But they will be better when we charge!

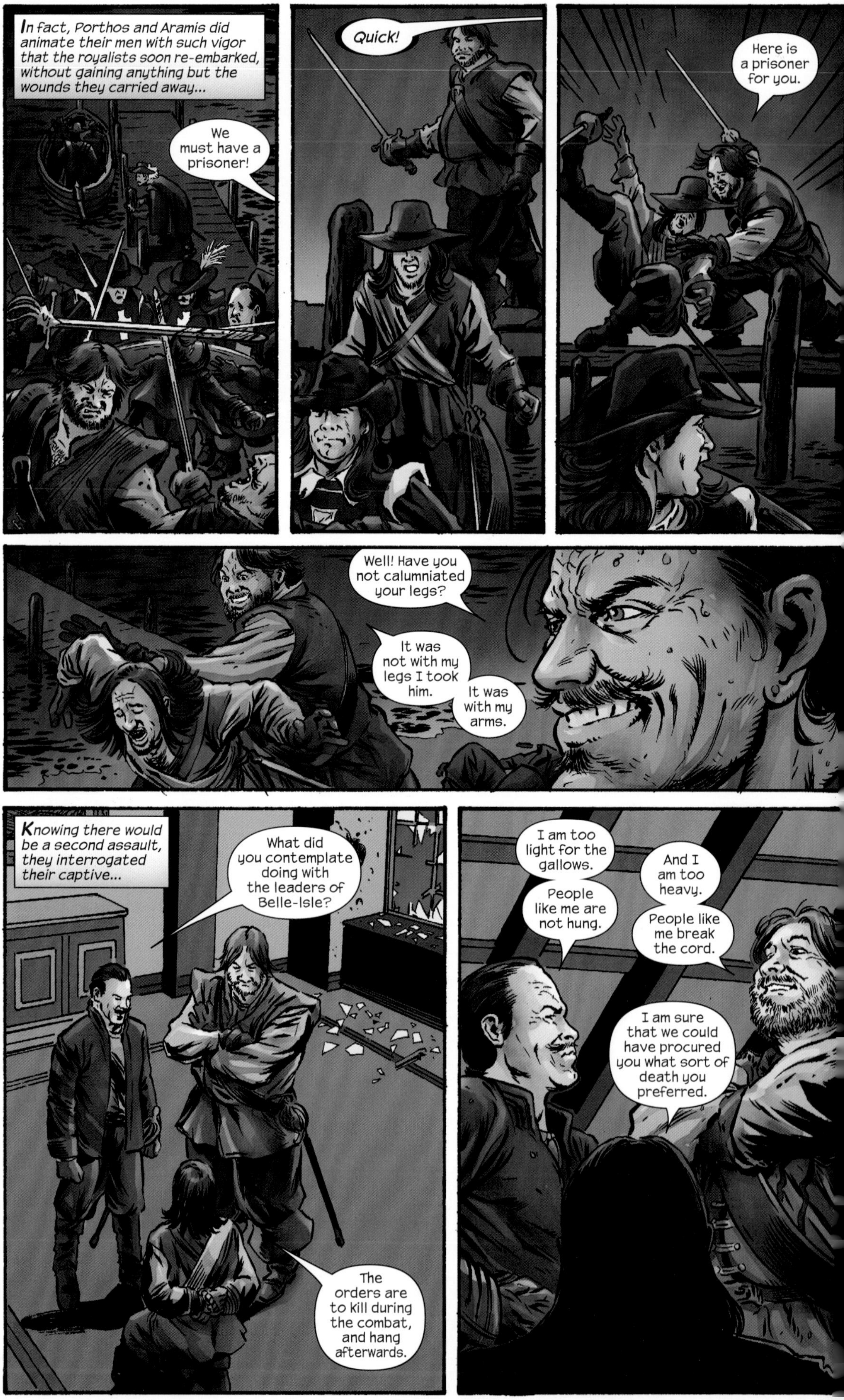
In fact, Porthos and Aramis did animate their men with such vigor that the royalists soon re-embarked, without gaining anything but the wounds they carried away...
We must have a prisoner!
Quick!
Here is a prisoner for you.
Well! Have you not calumniated your legs?
It was not with my legs I took him.
It was with my arms.
Knowing there would be a second assault, they interrogated their captive...
What did you contemplate doing with the leaders of Belle-Isle?
The orders are to kill during the combat, and hang afterwards.
I am too light for the gallows.
People like me are not hung.
And I am too heavy.
People like me break the cord.
I am sure that we could have procured you what sort of death you preferred.

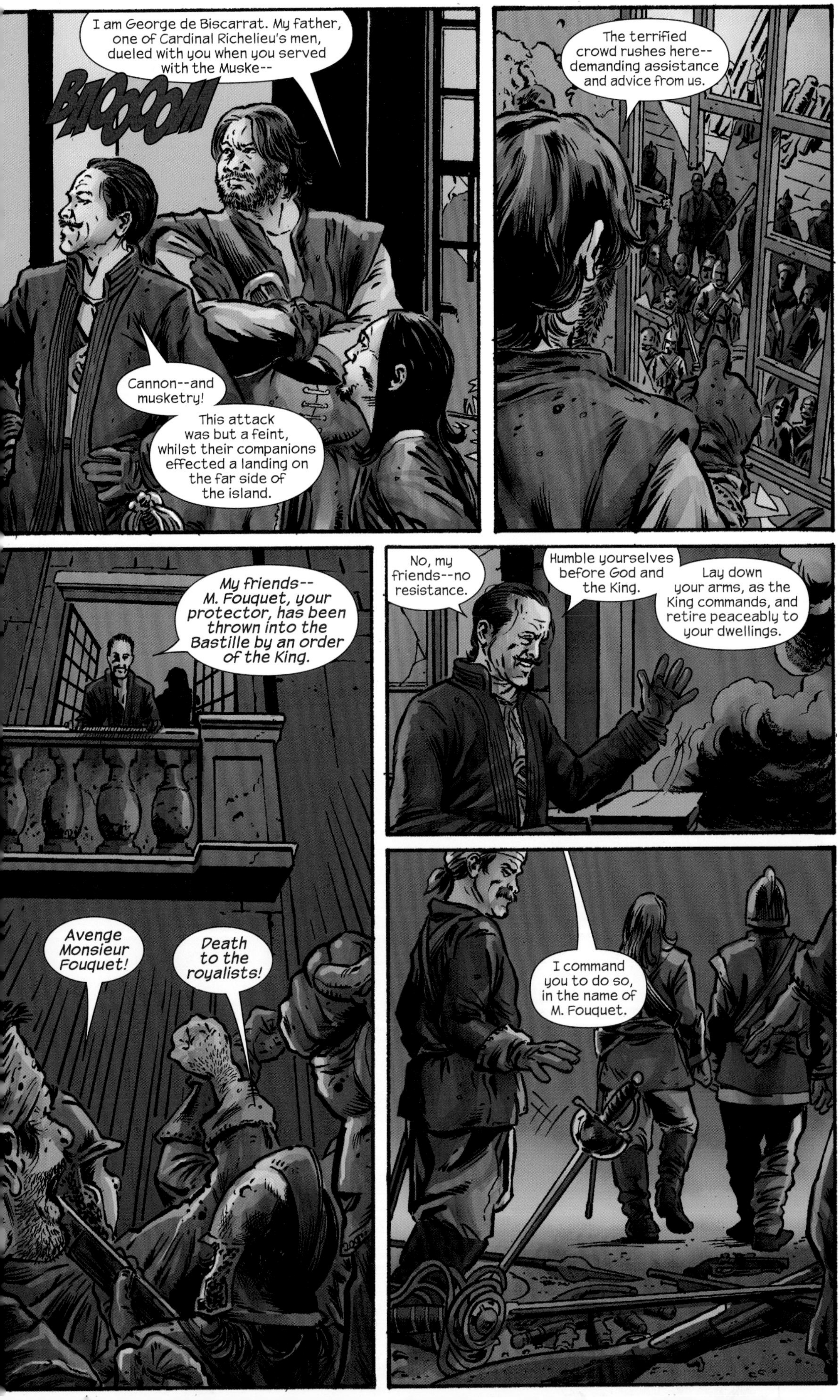
I am George de Biscarrat. My father, one of Cardinal Richelieu's men, dueled with you when you served with the Muske--
BADOOOM
Cannon--and musketry!
This attack was but a feint, whilst their companions effected a landing on the far side of the island.
The terrified crowd rushes here--demanding assistance and advice from us.
My friends-- M. Fouquet, your protector, has been thrown into the Bastille by an order of the King.
Avenge Monsieur Fouquet!
Death to the royalists!
No, my friends--no resistance.
Humble yourselves before God and the King.
Lay down your arms, as the King commands, and retire peaceably to your dwellings.
I command you to do so, in the name of M. Fouquet.

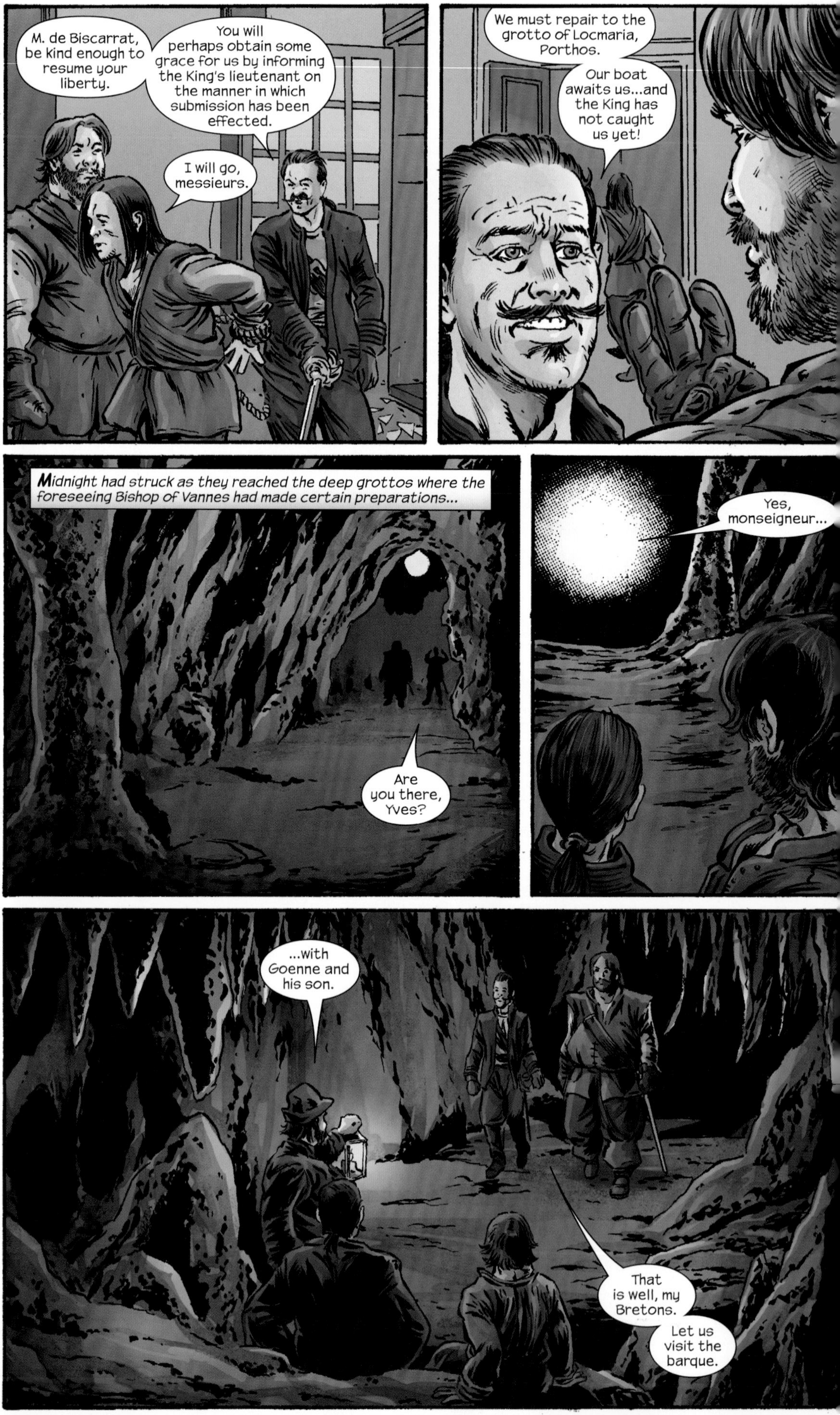

M. de Biscarrat, be kind enough to resume your liberty.
You will perhaps obtain some grace for us by informing the King's lieutenant on the manner in which submission has been effected.
I will go, messieurs.
We must repair to the grotto of Locmaria, Porthos.
Our boat awaits us...and the King has not caught us yet!
Midnight had struck as they reached the deep grottos where the foreseeing Bishop of Vannes had made certain preparations...
Are you there, Yves?
Yes, monseigneur...
...with Goenne and his son.
That is well, my Bretons.
Let us visit the barque.

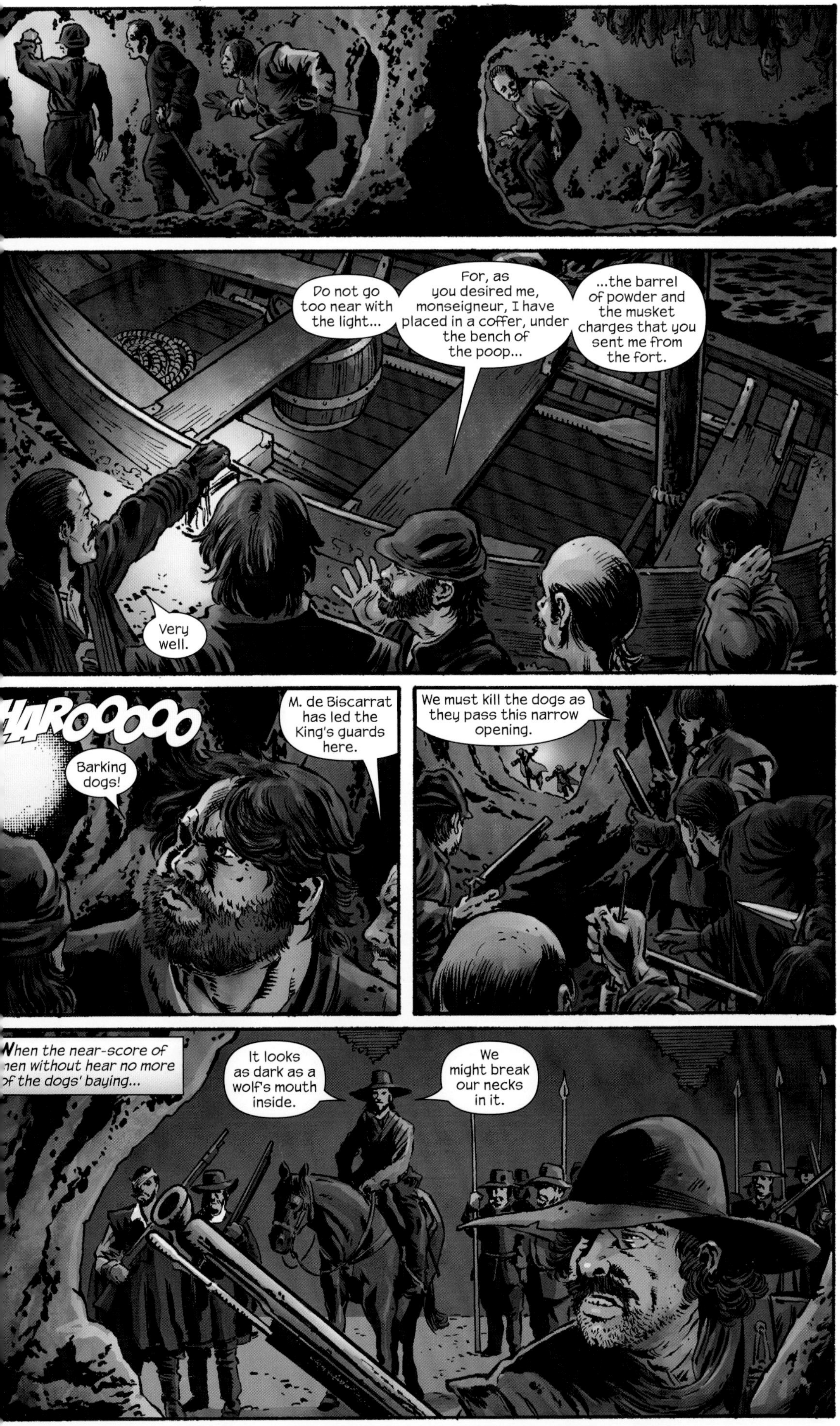

Do not go too near with the light...
For, as you desired me, monseigneur, I have placed in a coffer, under the bench of the poop...
...the barrel of powder and the musket charges that you sent me from the fort.
Very well.
HAROOOOO
Barking dogs!
M. de Biscarrat has led the King's guards here.
We must kill the dogs as they pass this narrow opening.
When the near-score of men without hear no more of the dogs' baying...
It looks as dark as a wolf's mouth inside.
We might break our necks in it.

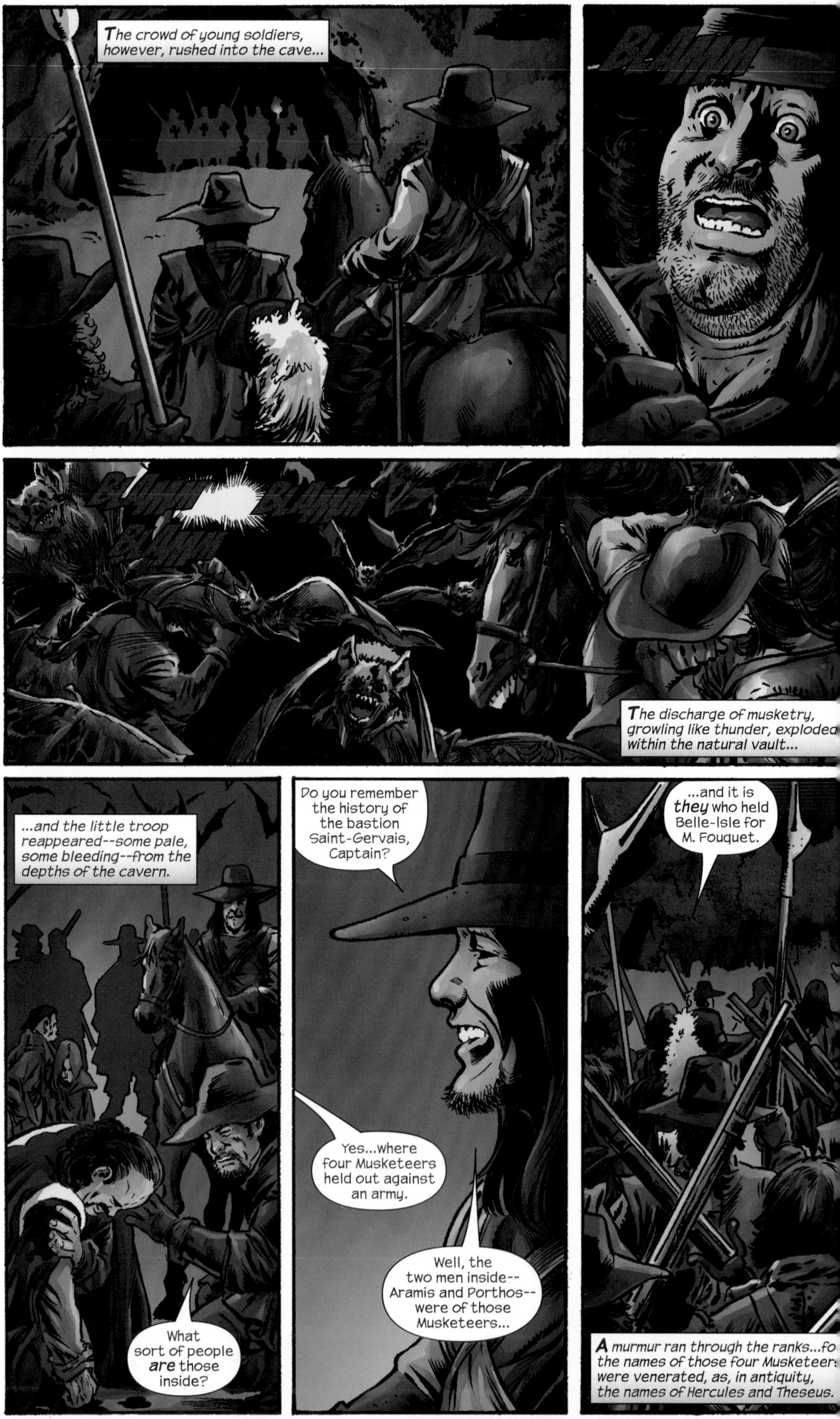
The crowd of young soldiers, however, rushed into the cave...
The discharge of musketry, growling like thunder, exploded within the natural vault...
...and the little troop reappeared--some pale, some bleeding--from the depths of the cavern.
What sort of people are those inside?
Do you remember the history of the bastion Saint-Gervais, Captain?
Yes...where four Musketeers held out against an army.
Well, the two men inside-- Aramis and Porthos-- were of those Musketeers...
...and it is they who held Belle-Isle for M. Fouquet.
A murmur ran through the ranks...fo the names of those four Musketeers were venerated, as, in antiquity, the names of Hercules and Theseus.

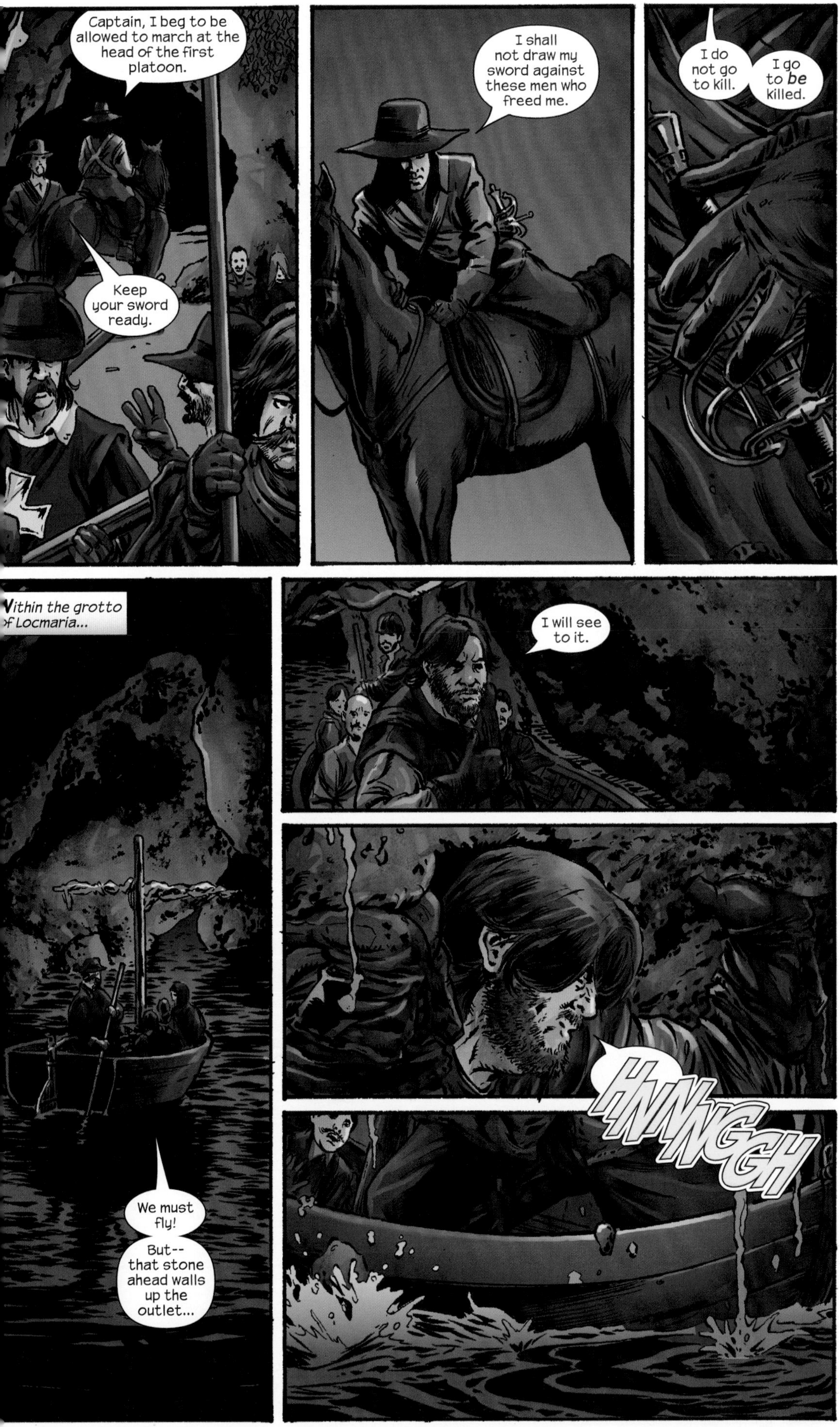
Captain, I beg to be allowed to march at the head of the first platoon.
Keep your sword ready.
I shall not draw my sword against these men who freed me.
I do not go to kill.
I go to ***be*** killed.
Within the grotto of Locmaria...
We must fly!
But-- that stone ahead walls up the outlet...
I will see to it.
HNNNGGH

HRRRRRHH

SPLWNSSH

Daylight.

Prepare for an assault!

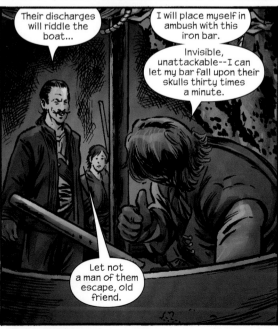

Their discharges will riddle the boat...

I will place myself in ambush with this iron bar.

Invisible, unattackable--I can let my bar fall upon their skulls thirty times a minute.

Let not a man of them escape, old friend.

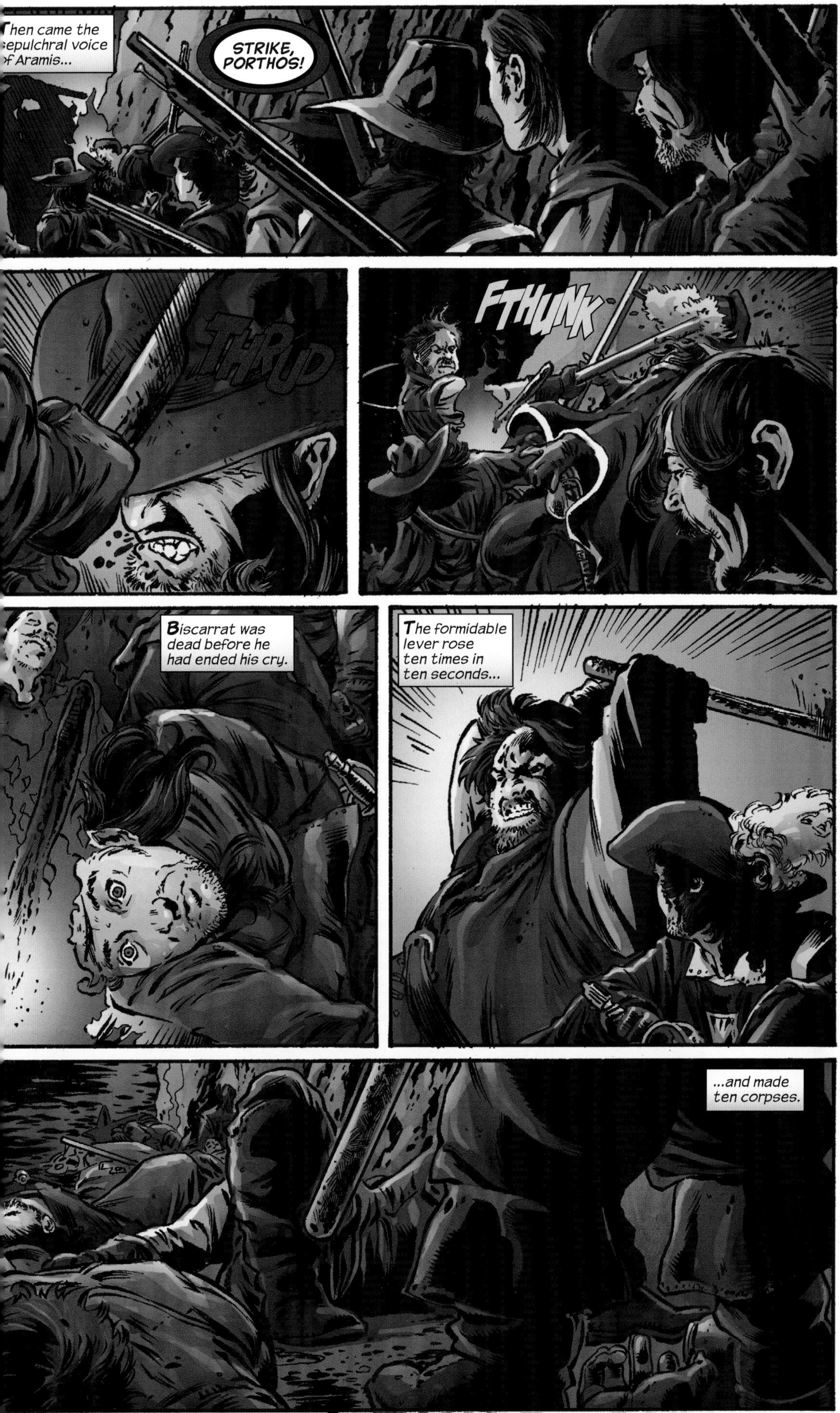
Then came the sepulchral voice of Aramis...
STRIKE, PORTHOS!
THRUD
FTHUNK
Biscarrat was dead before he had ended his cry.
The formidable lever rose ten times in ten seconds...
...and made ten corpses.

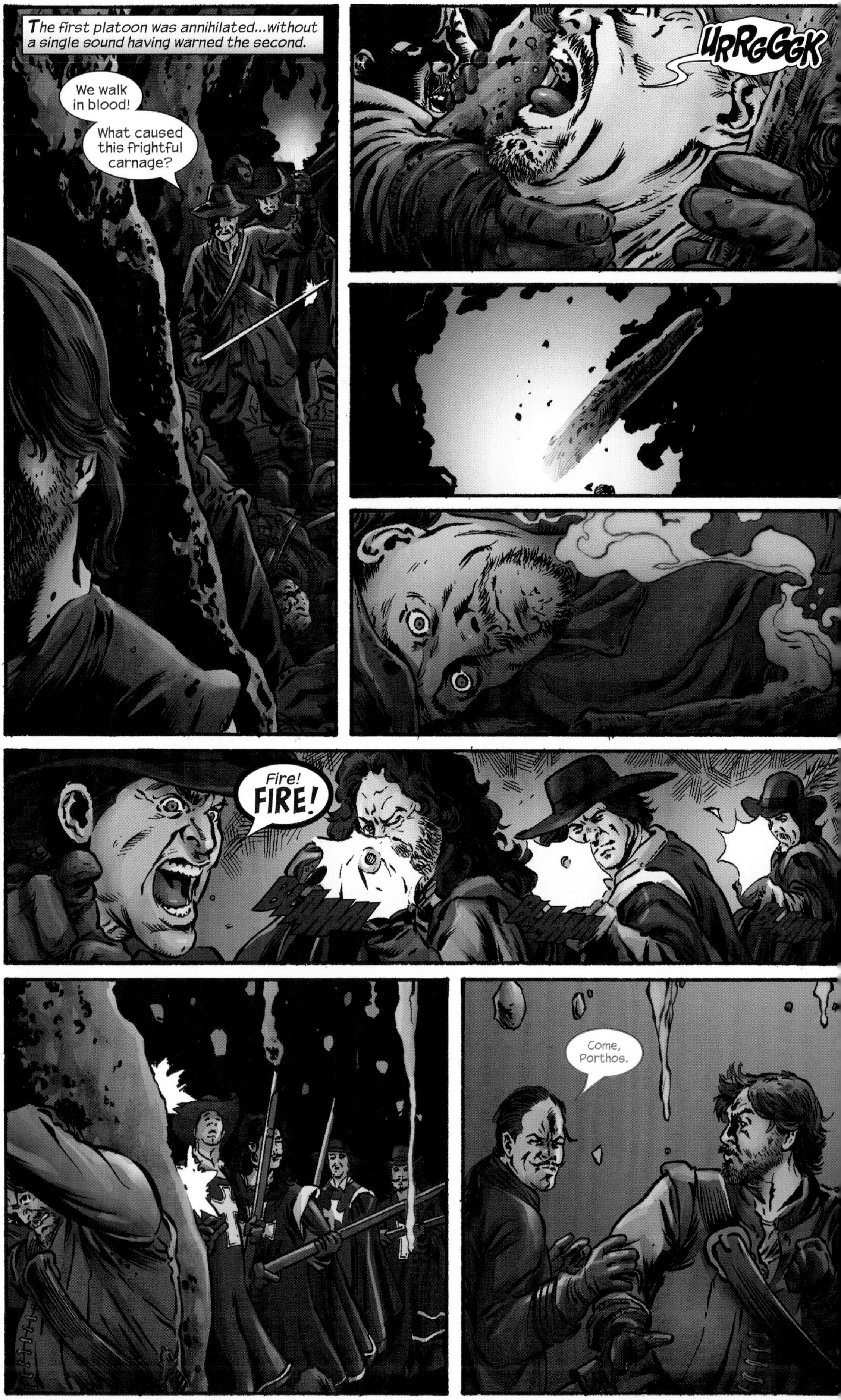
The first platoon was annihilated...without a single sound having warned the second.
We walk in blood!
What caused this frightful carnage?
URRGGGK
Fire! FIRE!
Come, Porthos.

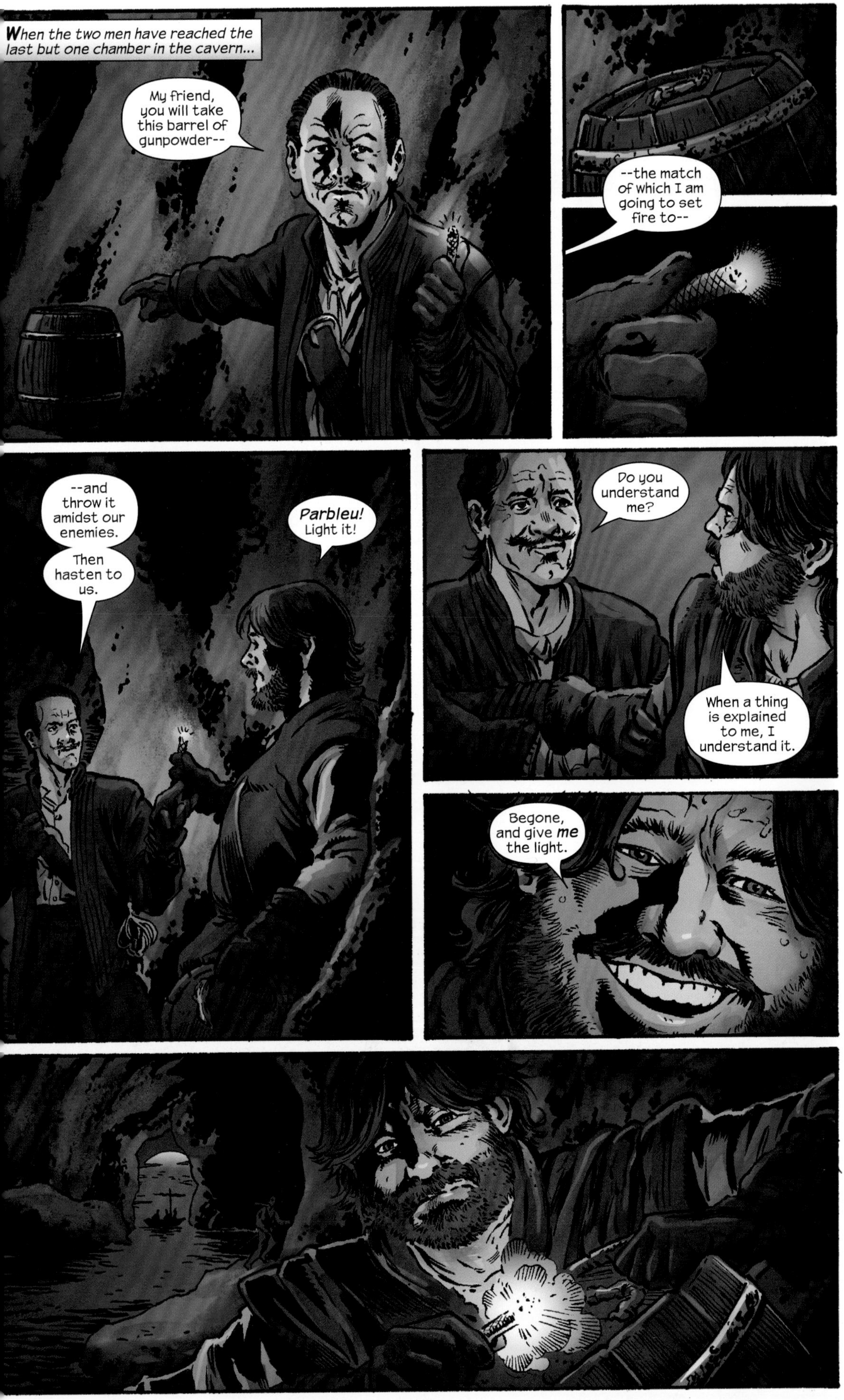
When the two men have reached the last but one chamber in the cavern...
My friend, you will take this barrel of gunpowder--
--the match of which I am going to set fire to--
--and throw it amidst our enemies.
Then hasten to us.
Parbleu! Light it!
Do you understand me?
When a thing is explained to me, I understand it.
Begone, and give me the light.

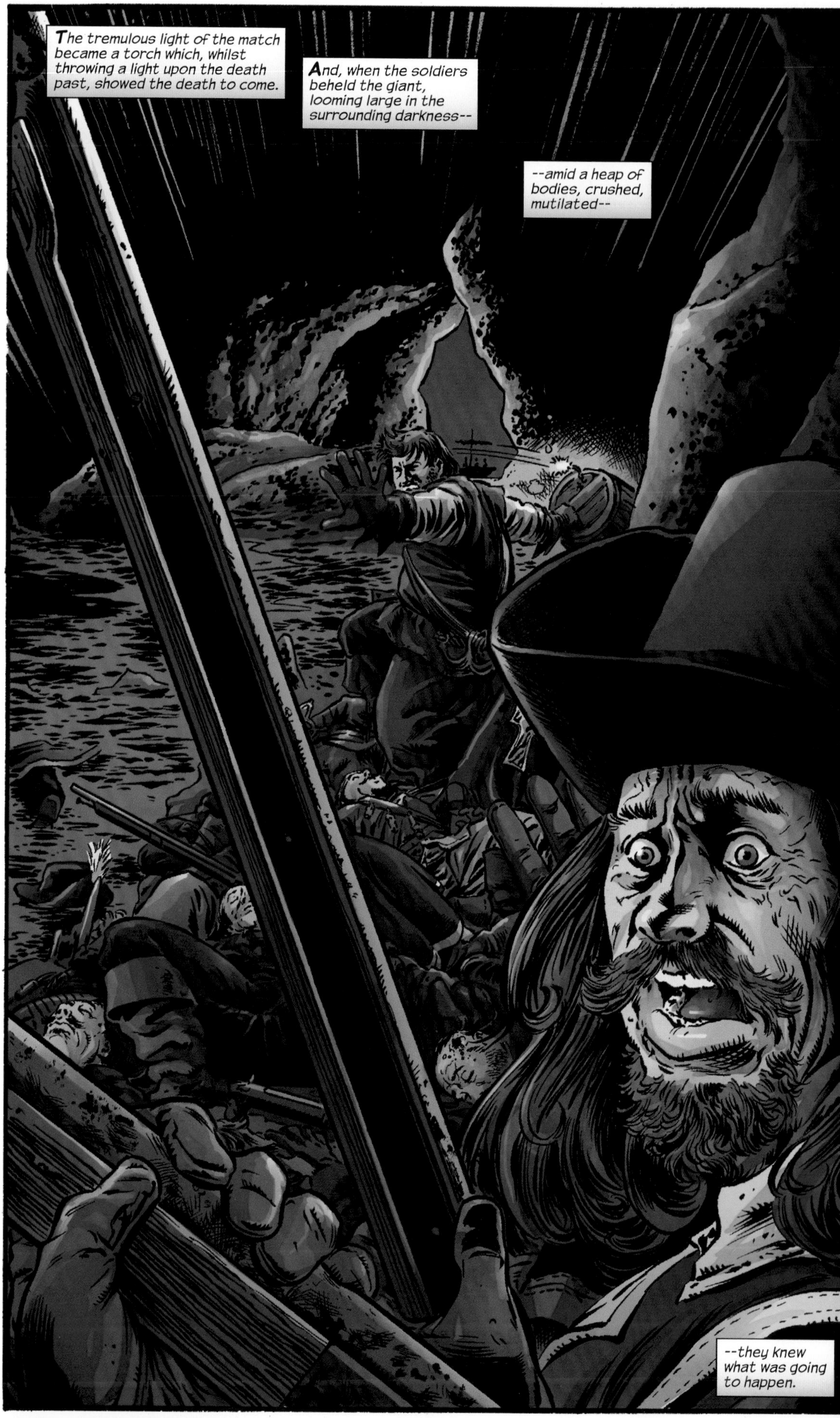
The tremulous light of the match became a torch which, whilst throwing a light upon the death past, showed the death to come.
And, when the soldiers beheld the giant, looming large in the surrounding darkness--
--amid a heap of bodies, crushed, mutilated--
--they knew what was going to happen.

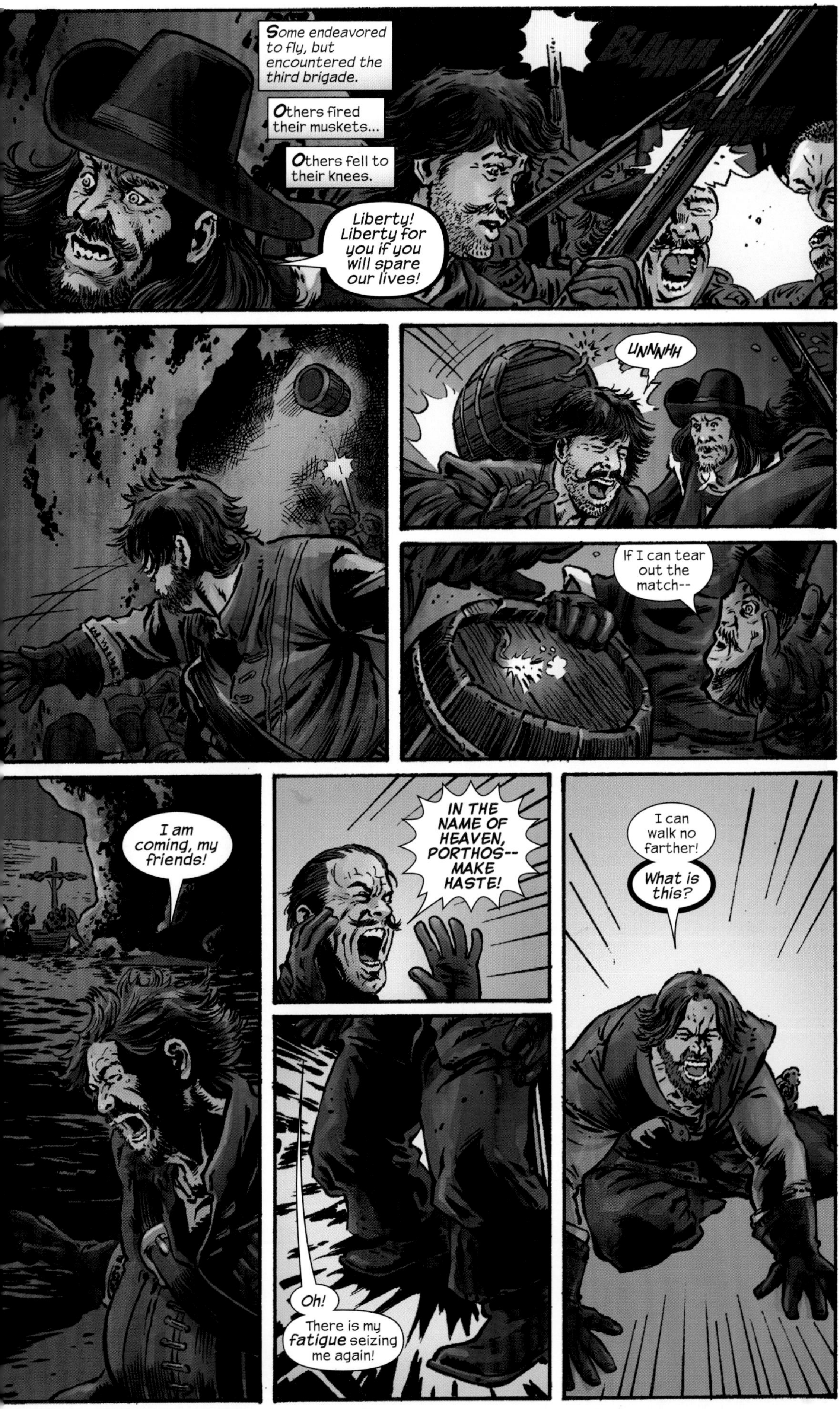
Some endeavored to fly, but encountered the third brigade.
Others fired their muskets...
Others fell to their knees.
Liberty! Liberty for you if you will spare our lives!
UNNNHH
If I can tear out the match--
I am coming, my friends!
IN THE NAME OF HEAVEN, PORTHOS-- MAKE HASTE!
Oh!
There is my fatigue seizing me again!
I can walk no farther!
What is this?

The shock of the explosion seemed to restore to Porthos the strength he had lost...

And he extended his vast hands to the right and left to repulse the falling rocks...

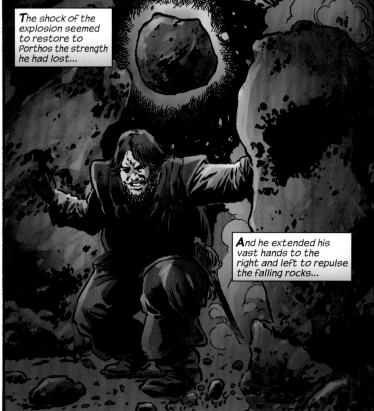

WATCH OUT PORTHOS!

ARRRRHH

But a third granite mass sank between his two shoulders...

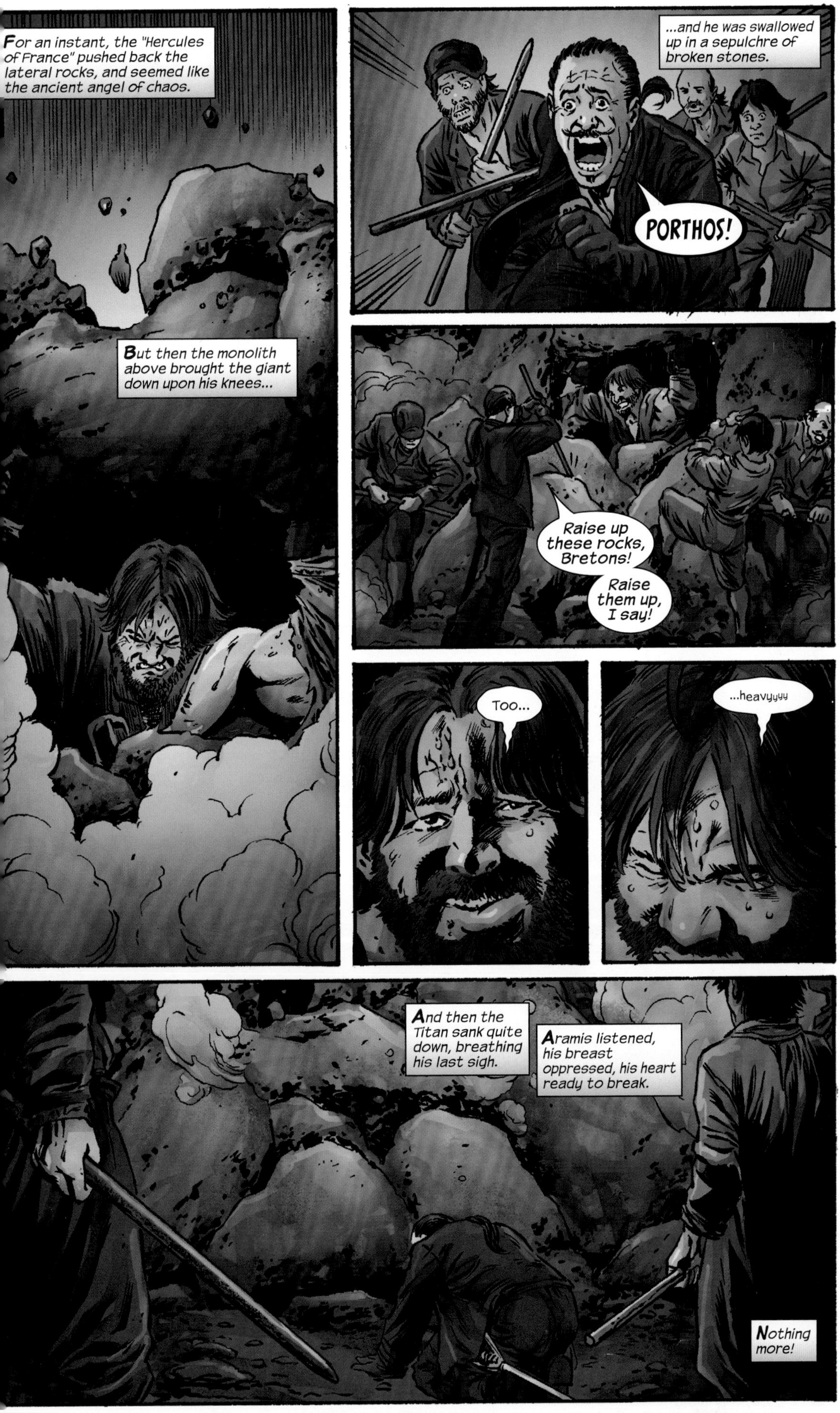
For an instant, the "Hercules of France" pushed back the lateral rocks, and seemed like the ancient angel of chaos.
But then the monolith above brought the giant down upon his knees...
...and he was swallowed up in a sepulchre of broken stones.
PORTHOS!
Raise up these rocks, Bretons!
Raise them up, I say!
Too...
...heavyyyy
And then the Titan sank quite down, breathing his last sigh.
Aramis listened, his breast oppressed, his heart ready to break.
Nothing more!

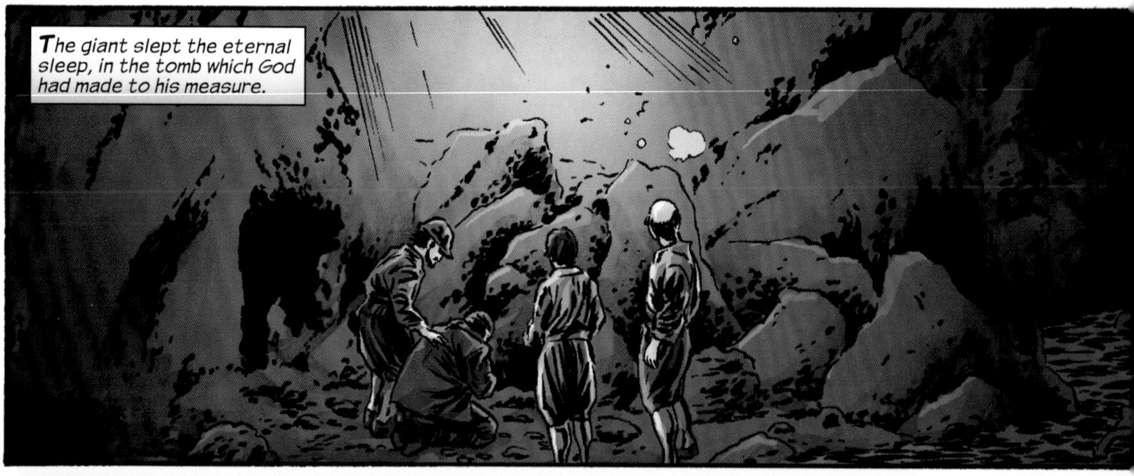
The giant slept the eternal sleep, in the tomb which God had made to his measure.

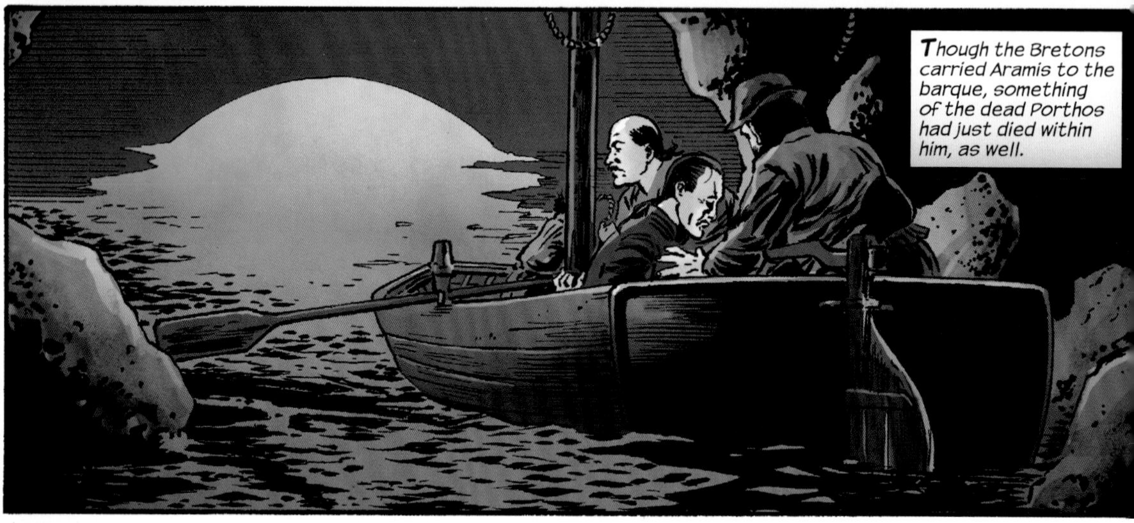
Though the Bretons carried Aramis to the barque, something of the dead Porthos had just died within him, as well.

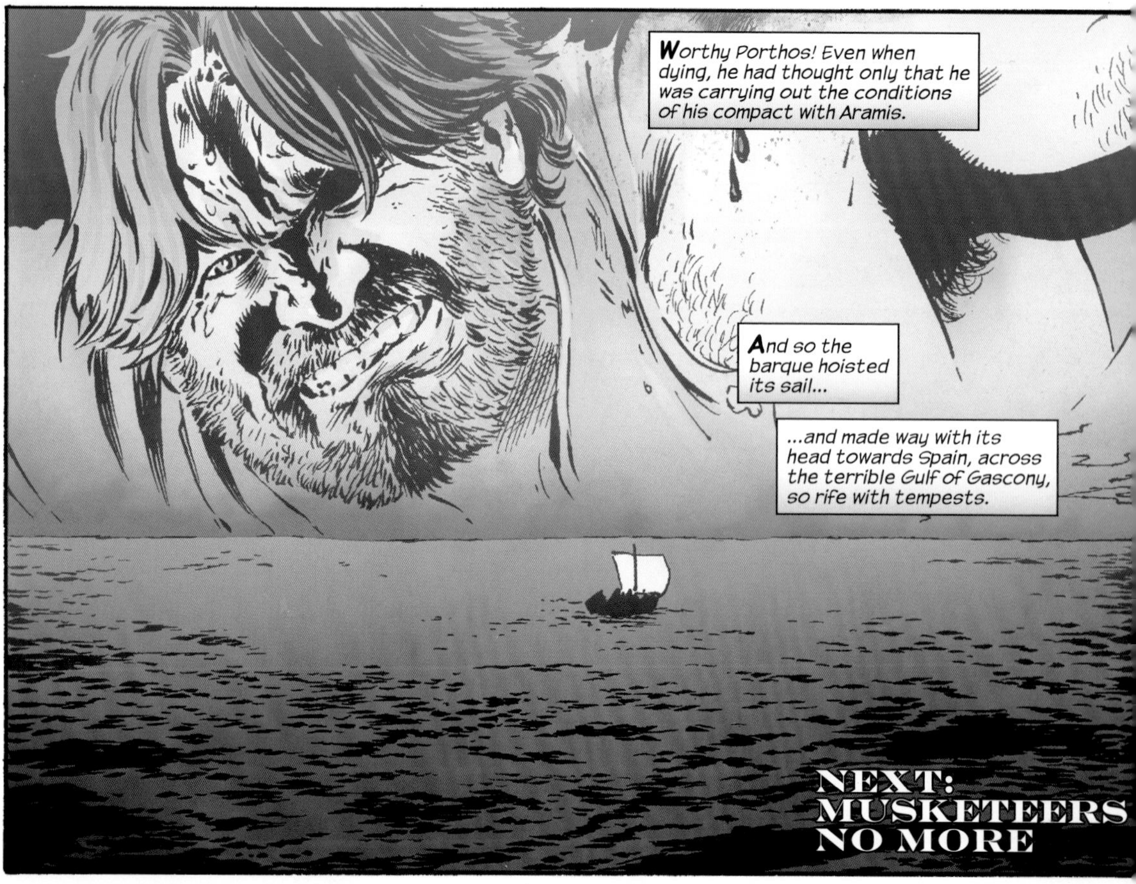
Worthy Porthos! Even when dying, he had thought only that he was carrying out the conditions of his compact with Aramis.
And so the barque hoisted its sail...
...and made way with its head towards Spain, across the terrible Gulf of Gascony, so rife with tempests.
NEXT: MUSKETEERS NO MORE